Eli
by Bill Peet

Houghton Mifflin Company   Boston

With gratitude to my
good friend and neighbor
Dr. Harold Marcus

Library of Congress Cataloging in Publication Data

Peet, Bill.
  Eli.

  SUMMARY: A proud but decrepit lion learns a lesson
about friendship from the vultures he despises.
  [1. Lions—Fiction. 2. Vultures—Fiction.
3. Friendship—Fiction.] I. Title.
PZ7.P353Ek [E]   77-17500
ISBN 0-395-26454-5 (rnf.)
ISBN 0-395-36611-9 (pbk.)

Printed in the United States of America

WOZ   20 19 18 17 16 15 14 13 12

Once upon a time there was a lion named Eli who lived in the faraway land of Kumbumbazango. He was a decrepit old cat with a scruffy mop of mane, and most of the thunder had gone out of his roar. Now, after many long years as a proud king of beasts, the old lion had finally become as meek as a mouse.

Whenever the other lions gathered for a feast Eli didn't dare join in. It was much too rough, one big snarling free-for-all with every cat for himself. So the old fellow waited until the lions all had their share and the hyenas and jackals had eaten their fill of the leftovers.

Finally Eli joined a squawking, squabbling flock of vultures for what scraps and small bits he could find in the clutter of bones. The noisy birds were a nagging nuisance to the old lion, and he tried to avoid them as best he could. Whenever a vulture ventured too close, Eli scared the bird off with a rumbling growl.

"An old cat like me can't afford to be choosy," he grumbled, "or too proud to have dinner with these beggars. So I must put up with their bad manners and their awful squawking, but I'll never make friends with the lowly creatures. Not as long as I live."

After a time Eli was able to ignore the birds by pretending they weren't there, just as if he were having dinner alone.

Then one day an old vulture let out such a terrible ear-splitting scream the lion shivered and shook all the way to his toes. The bird kept screaming and screeching until Eli couldn't stand any more, and suddenly he turned on her in a snarling fury.

But when he realized she was screaming for help, that a jackal had caught her by a wing and was about to drag her away, Eli took pity on the poor bird.

In one frantic leap and with a wild swing of a paw, Eli caught the jackal with a clout to the snout that sent the little rascal yelping away with his tail between his legs.

Once the old bird was free she was surrounded by a dozen fussy, fretting friends. "Vera! Vera!" they cried. "You poor thing! Are you hurt? Are you hurt?"

"Not in the least," said Vera. "Thanks to that dear old lion."

"He is a dear!" the birds exclaimed. "One prince of a fellow!"

All at once the vultures were flocking around Eli, singing his praises in loud screechy voices.

"Leo's a jolly good fellow. Leo's a jolly good fellow! Leo's a jolly good fell*ooo*w! Oh what a great lion is he!"

"My name is *not* Leo," snarled the miserable lion. "I'm Eli, and I'm *not* great! There's nothing great about saving a worthless old bird. It was nothing at all. SO FORGET IT!"

But the vultures were never going to forget Eli, not after such a great act of kindness to one of their flock. To them he was a hero whether he liked it or not. And to the old lion's dismay the birds followed him wherever he went. If he took a morning stroll his faithful followers came fluttering along a short distance behind.

In the heat of the afternoon, when the old lion flopped down in the shade of his favorite tumbaba tree for a cat nap, the vultures were there too, roosting in the branches above.

"I see enough of these birds at dinnertime," grumbled Eli, "without being stuck with them from morning 'til night. Enough is enough! And I have an idea of how to get rid of the pests once and for all. I'll insult them. I'll call them all the meanest most horrible things I can think of. After that they'll never want to see me again."

Raising his voice to a rumble to make sure all the birds could hear, the lion let them have it. "You good-for-nothing grubby old bone-pickers! You flea-bitten beggars! You ugly old coots! You give me the creeps! Skeedaddle! Take off! Get a tree of your own! Leave me be!!!"

For a minute the vultures were so horrified by the sudden outburst they were left goggle-eyed and speechless. Finally Vera, the old bird Eli had rescued, spoke up. "I can't blame you for feeling this way," she said. "We are indeed creepy old things. We will do as you wish, and leave you be. But no matter what you say, we are still your friends, and in some way we old birds might prove to be useful someday."

That someday came surprisingly soon. It was the very next afternoon. Vera and her vulture friends were circling high above the plain
searching for leftovers when they spotted a band of Zoobangas armed
with spears sneaking along through the bush. Being ever so curious,
Vera swooped down for a better look, to discover that the men were
tracking a lion. The old bird guessed at once whose paw prints they
were, and she took off in a tizzy to warn the old cat.

Vera found the lion in his usual spot under the tumbaba tree deep in a cat nap.

"Eli! Eli!," screeched the frantic bird, "Wake up, old lion! Wake up! The Zoobangas are coming!"

"The Zoo whos?," mumbled the drowsy sleepy-eyed lion, "The Bang zooies?"

"The lion hunters. The men with the spears! They're hot on your trail!"

"Lion hunters? Spears?" wailed Eli, sitting up with a shiver of fright. "What'll I do? Where'll I go?!!"

"To the gumbazunka swamp! Quick! On your feet! Follow me!"

Off they went, with the frantic vulture fluttering ahead urging the lion to pick up the pace. "Faster! Faster! Shake your bones, old cat! Run scared! Lickety clip!!"

"I *am* running scared," yelled Eli, "but I can't lickety clip! My top speed is lumpity clumpity," and he kept lumpity-clumping along as fast as his gimpy old legs could carry him.

"There you go," cried Vera when they reached the edge of the swamp. "Wade out into that soup and scrunch down in the gunkazunk grass. The Zoobangas will never look for you there."

"No lion to look for," groaned Eli, "after those clopper-jawed crocodiles finish me off."

"Oh dear! Crocs all over the place! I forgot about those lousy lizards. Now you've got to hide somewhere else!"

"I'm not hiding," Eli muttered under his breath, "I'm a lion. And I'm going to be brave and act like a lion."

All at once the old lion exploded into a great snarling, roaring rage.
"I'll give them a battle!" he bellowed. "I'll give the Zoo-whoosits, or
whoever they are, a battle they'll never forget!" And he wheeled around
and went roaring off to meet the Zoobangas.

"No! No!" screeched the horrified vulture, as she came sailing after
him. "Stop! Stop! Don't you dare! You silly old cat!"

In a flick of an eye Vera caught up to the rampaging lion and cut loose with such a fierce peck on his snoot that Eli went rocking back on his heels.

"This is no time to be brave," the bird pleaded. "If you put up a fight you won't last a minute!"

"Then what'll I do?" growled Eli. "Act like a ninny? Roll over and play dead?"

"Yes! Yes!" cried Vera. "Great idea! Roll over and play dead! I mean it! Flop down! Play dead! Go ahead!"

"Like this?" asked Eli, sprawling out on his back in the weeds.

"Perfect!" cried Vera. "Just dandy! Now hold it! Don't you dare budge! Don't wiggle an ear or twitch one whisker! Stay put while I round up the rest of the act! I'll be back in a flash!"

In a flash the old vulture was back with her flock of bone-picking friends, and as they came swooping down on the play-acting lion Vera was shouting instructions. "Swarm all over him! Peck! Peck! Peck! Pitch in, everyone! Make it look real! But don't get too rough!"

In an instant the vultures were all over Eli, pecking away at their make-believe feast, squawking and squabbling to make it look real.

In the next instant the Zoobangas came charging over a hill all set to attack. But when they caught sight of the sprawled-out lion swarmed over by a mob of squawking, pecking vultures they staggered to a halt and gaped in surprise.

"How can it be?" they wondered. "Simba! The great cat! Done in! What happened? What got poor old Simba?"

"Speared by a rhino," muttered the chief, "or snake bit. No telling what. Anyway, we can't fight a dead lion, so let's call it a day. Hup! Ho! Let's go!"

Then, grouching and grumping about their bad luck, the Zoobangas turned and went trotting back over the hill.

"Ho! Ho! I do believe we fooled 'em," cackled Vera, "but hold everything while I make sure they're gone for good."

And she sailed high into the sky to keep a sharp eye on the Zoobangas. She kept watching until they were no more than tiny dots in the distance. Then cheerily Vera sang out, "All clear! All clear! Come to life old Eli! Stand up and take a bow! That was some fantastic act! Just super!"

"That was no act," said Eli. "I was too scared to move. Scared stiff! You birds did all the acting. You even fooled me. For a minute I thought you might peck me to pieces. What a great bunch of fakers!"

"No! No! Please!" Vera protested. "Don't praise us too much or we might become proud. If we ever get too snooty to eat leftovers we vultures would go hungry. Just treat us with a little respect, and be grateful you have so many good friends to count on."

Eli was indeed grateful for his fine feathered friends, and when he invited them to come back to roost in his tumbaba tree they happily accepted.

After that, whenever the old lion flopped down for a cat nap he peered up into the branches to make sure they were there. The old lion discovered that life was not nearly so dreary and lonely with a tree full of friends for company. And even if they were a bunch of old bone-pickers, Eli was ever so proud of them.